NORMIE

Jane Carroll

CARROLL, Jane

Normie

Kate vindt een jonge kaketoe, die ze
verzorgt en hij groeit op tot een
gezellig speelkameraadje. Maar dan
verschijnt een groep wilde kaketoe's
en hij vliegt met ze mee.

NORMIE

Jane Carroll

Illustrated by Lucinda Hunnam

WALTER McVITTY
BOOKS

First published 1989 by
WALTER McVITTY BOOKS
27 Hereford Street, Glebe, NSW 2037, Australia
Text Copyright ©, Jane Carroll, 1989
Illustrations copyright, ©, Lucinda Hunnam, 1989
Text set in 14/16 pt Century by The Type Shop Pty Limited,
Five Dock, NSW
Printed by The Globe Press, Brunswick, Vic.

ISBN 0 949183 22 9 (Special paperback edition printed for members
of Ashton Scholastic Book Club only, and not for general sale.)

To Elizabeth
and the Thursday morning class

1

Flycatcher

"WAIT a minute, Clarrie!"
Kate Harman sat at the back of the school bus and scribbled last night's homework into *Maths is Magical — Year 4*. Clarrie, the driver, waited. The others were already tumbling and chattering down the steps. They ran with bags and cases thumping along a concrete path to the little bush school.

Maths was *not* magical. Tadpoles turning into frogs was magical. Kate watched them in the aquarium she had made in Dad's old milk bucket. Her collection of blue glass from the rubbish tip was magical, the way it gleamed like real jewels. Finding a brolga's nest would be magical. Perhaps dreams were magical too, because sometimes they came true.

But writing sums into a red book was not magical. It was *boring*. Kate slapped the book shut and pushed up the aisle.

"'Bye, Clarrie," she said.

"See yuh, Darlin'."

Clarrie smiled and straightened his arms on the steering wheel.

At the doorway Kate stopped and glanced around the playground. Doongara Primary School sat, surrounded by pepper trees and gum plantations, in a flat paddock. It was a single weatherboard classroom, painted cream, with a verandah and a steep corrugated iron roof, like the sunshade Mum wore when she played tennis. The big kids were playing cricket in the back paddock. The little ones squealed and shouted in their pepper tree cubby.

And there was The Gang.

Kate clutched the bus's shiny handrail as if she were frozen to it. There were only three girls in The Gang, but they were so big they were scarier than ten ordinary kids. Michelle was the biggest. She swung around a verandah post, talking with Sharon and Cynthia.

Wish Andy was here, Kate thought. But her brother had rushed to join the game of cricket before the bell rang.

"You all right?" Clarrie said at last.

Kate nodded, though she looked as pale as putty. Her chest felt tight and her heart thumped like the Harmans' old fridge.

"Off you go then, Love."

She clutched her school case under her arm, took a deep breath, and climbed three big steps down from the bus. As she walked she kept her eyes fixed on the garden beds beside the path. They were diamond-

shaped beds with brick borders and straggly iris in them.

"Here comes Flycatcher!"

Kate winced at the sound of Michelle's voice. She shut her mouth and kept her feet following each other up the path. It was hard to breathe through her nose. Adenoids, Mum said. The doctor had taken them out when she was four, but she still breathed through her mouth. So Michelle called her Flycatcher.

The girls clattered towards her and surrounded her, so close she could feel them breathing on her.

"Caught any flies this morning, Flycatcher?"

"Are they yummy and crunchy?"

"Do their wings get stuck in your throat?"

They laughed. Michelle grabbed Kate's shoulder and shoved her pudgy face closer to the smaller girl. "Shut ya mouth have ya, Flycatcher?"

"Leave me alone!"

Kate wriggled from Michelle's grip. She dropped her case and it crashed onto the concrete path and burst open. *Maths is Magical* flopped onto its spine and a green apple rolled into the iris bed. Kate stared at it. Tears prickled her eyes and the apple went blurry.

"Buzz-z-z-z-z. The flies'll get out."

Kate scrabbled on the ground, stuffed her things back into the case, and dived through the circle. She half walked, half ran up the path.

"Flycatcher, Flycatcher," The Gang chanted behind her.

*   *   *

Andy was wearing his cricket hat. He always wore his cricket hat, even at bedtime. It was signed by five of the Australian team and it was the best thing he owned. The hat, once white, was now a patchy pale brown, but Mum was not allowed to wash it in case the signatures came off. Mum was not allowed to *touch* it.

Andy hooked his long, bony thumbs into his shorts and watched the bowler trundle over the grass. Kate sneaked up beside him and he glanced down at her.

"What's the matter?" he asked.

"Big bullies!'' She swiped angrily at the tears which spilt down her cheeks and told him what had happened.

"It wouldn't matter if you shut your mouth and blew bubbles out your ears," said Andy. "Michelle would still pick on you."

"Why?"

"Dunno. P'raps it's because you're the only kid in Fourth Class."

Andy ran forward, scooped up the ball, and hurled it back to the wicket keeper. He trotted back to where Kate stood, twisting a silky brown pigtail around her fingers.

"She's just a mean old cow. Or a *toad*," he said.

"Fat and blotchy," giggled Kate.

"With googly eyes."

Andy rolled his eyes and crossed them. Then he grinned and gave his sister's arm a friendly punch.

"Don't take any notice of old Toad Features."

"You sound just like Mum. I do try to 'ignore' her. But she still won't leave me alone."

Andy took off his hat and rubbed his hair, making it look like a just-opened bale of straw. He replaced the hat carefully and kept his eyes on the game.

"What are you going to do?" he asked.

"I don't know," Kate sighed. "What *can* I do?"

2

A Pet Show

*D*ING-a-ling-a-ling-a-ling-a-ling!
Mr Lodge stood on the verandah and rang the bell.

"I bags bowl at playtime!" yelled Andy, as everyone ran to line up.

"Good morning, girls and boys," said the teacher, smiling beneath his bristly moustache.

"Good mor-ning, Mis-ter Lodge," droned the seventeen pupils of Doongara Primary School.

"Right," said Mr Lodge, and felt his moustache with the back of his finger. "Lead the way please, Andrew and Michelle. Andrew, take your hat off!"

The children filed into a big rectangular room. Two large fans hung from the high ceiling. On hot, sticky days Kate watched the fans whirring and imagined what would happen if one whizzed right off the ceiling. It might fly down and chop Michelle into chunks.

Tables and chairs clustered at one end of the room. Yellow work trays slotted into shelves under the windows. Mr Lodge's desk sat in a corner. He lined his pens up along its front — blue, red, black — and he pounced on anyone who touched them, his heavy hand crashing down on the curious little fingers.

At the other end of the room a bright green carpet covered the floor and a television stared from one corner. A mobile of papier-maché budgerigars flew crookedly from the light.

Kate liked the Reading Corner best. It had bean bags to sit in and she could hide behind the bookshelves.

"Right. Sit on the carpet please, everyone. This morning I have something exciting to tell you."

Mr Lodge checked the register, as if he were not the least bit excited.

They sat cross-legged on the bright green square. The sun shone through the window and lit up specks of dust in the air. It made square patterns of light and shadow on the children and the floor.

"Right," said Mr Lodge, and touched his moustache for the seventh time that morning. "For the past two weeks we've all worked hard on our theme of . . . ?"

"Pets!"

"That's right. And we still have lots more work to do. But what about a special event for the end of our unit?"

"Yes!"

"What about . . ." He leant forward. His eyes flickered over the upturned faces. ". . .a Pet Show?"

"Yes!"

"Hands up who could bring a pet?"

Sixteen hands shot up.

"What about you, Kate? Surely you could bring a pet. You're always finding animals to mother."

"Yes, Mr Lodge, but . . ."

"She could bring pet flies," whispered Michelle. The Gang looked at each other and sniggered behind their hands.

"What about that baby possum you found?" said Mr Lodge.

"She died."

"I'm sorry to hear that, Kate. But you live on a farm. You have lots of animals at home. Couldn't you bring another pet?"

"I suppose so."

Kate put her hand half way up. She loved the animals at Corella, the Harmans' farm — Bob and Sparkie and Socks, the dogs; her pony, Silver; the poddy calves and the pet lambs — and even Mum's precious chooks. But since Squeak had died she did not have a pet of her very own. Squeak had been so

soft and cuddly, and so funny, with her brown button eyes and her clever paws that could hold a piece of apple while she ate it.

"I'll bring Nibs," said Lucy, her dark curls bouncing. "She's my rabbit. You *wouldn't* bring that carpet snake would you, Matthew?"

"Cyril? Of course I'll bring old Cyril!" Matthew grinned and made his ears stick out even further than usual. He was in Year Three with Lucy.

"Can I bring a sheep?" Andy asked. He would bring Baa, who was once a poddy lamb and was now a motherly three-year-old ewe. Baa still tapped her hooves on the back gate every morning for a saucepan of milk.

"What about a horse?" said Brian, who went to Pony Club every Saturday.

"I'll bring Tess," said Michelle, and for a minute her face looked gentle and smiling. Tess was a black and white border collie, rather broad after having six litters of puppies. Michelle loved the old sheep-dog more than anything or anybody.

"Right," said Mr Lodge. "Let's make it three weeks

from today — the last Friday in October."

"Will there be prizes?" Andy asked.

"Yes, I think so," said Mr Lodge. "What about a prize for the pet with the biggest ears? Or the longest tail?"

"The smallest pet," squeaked Anna, who was the smallest child in the school. She would bring her pet mouse, Pinkie.

"The scariest!" said Matthew, showing the whites of his eyes.

Everyone laughed — except Kate. Kate was not listening. She twined her pigtail around her fingers and gazed out the window. If only I could bring Squeak to the Pet Show, she wished. Nobody else has a pet possum. It's not fair. Why did she have to die? Everyone would have crowded around us and said, "Isn't she *soft?* Isn't she *clever?* Can I have a hold? Can I give her a piece of my apple? *Pleeease* Kate?" No-one would have called me Flycatcher. And all the prizes Squeak would have won — the most beautiful eyes. . .the fluffiest tail. . .the softest fur. . .!

"Kate, stop dreaming! We have work to do!" Mr Lodge's moustache bristled and his eyes glared.

Kate sighed, and followed the others to the work tables.

3

Kate Finds Something

"**A**ND THE prize for the most unusual pet goes to. . .''

Kate snuggled down in bed and tried to finish her dream. She had brought a monster to the Pet Show and it had just wrapped its thirteen hairy legs around Michelle. . .

Her eyes flipped open. It was Saturday! She turned onto her back, clasped her hands under her head, and sighed happily. Two long lovely days at home! Outside, a pair of topknot pigeons cooed over their nest in the scraggy pine tree. A magpie carolled from a currajong tree. The sky was palest blue.

Kate threw back the bedclothes and swung her feet onto the polished wooden floor. At the other end of the sleepout a hump snored gently under a patchy, pale brown cricket hat. She took two steps and one leap and landed on it.

"Go away, you pest!"

Kate bounced harder. "Come on Andy, get up! Let's go for a ride."

"You never want to get up on school mornings." Andy rubbed his hair and looked under the bed for some clothes.

Kate dressed and ran to the kitchen. She got cornflakes, peanut butter and apricot jam from the pantry. From the fridge she took a heavy jug of milk, and home-made butter with lines on it from the wooden butter pats. Kate loved making butter with Mum. She made toast and set the breakfast on the pine table which stood near the kitchen window. The scent of wisteria blossom wafted through the open window and mingled with the smell of warm toast.

Andy pushed through the swing door and clomped in his riding boots to the table.

"Let's go to Dead Tree," he said, spreading dollops of butter, peanut butter and jam onto a piece of toast. He bit into it, inspected the teeth marks he had made, then mumbled, "There are cows and calves in that paddock. We can check them for Dad."

"That's where we saw the goanna! We might find some baby ducks on the dam today."

Andy scraped his chair from the table. "You'll find something, Kate. You always do."

* * *

They rode across wide, flat paddocks. The sun warmed Kate's back through her red jacket, but the air was still tingly on her face and hands. Silver swished jauntily through waves of grass, and her white tail flew behind, like a flag on a ship. Kate let the reins swing and hummed to herself. She shut her eyes and smelt ripening grass.

"Race you to the tree!"

Andy shot past, making Silver shy, and headed for a solitary, long-dead tree. Kate grabbed the reins and leant forward. Silver's legs bunched underneath her and she burst into a gallop. They rode like the wind, making ripples in a silvery sea of grass.

"Beat you!"

Andy turned and laughed as he flashed first past the tree. Galahs lifted shrieking from its hollows, then turned their pink breasts to the sun and wheeled away.

"You had a start!" Kate tried to catch her breath. The horses' sides heaved and the hair on their necks curled damply.

"Andy, look!"

She kicked both feet out of the stirrups and dropped to the ground. "Oh — the poor little thing."

"I knew you'd find something. Let's have a look."

"It's just a baby."

Kate knelt and parted the long grass at the foot of the tree. Two round, shiny eyes stared up at her from a clump of pink and grey feathers. She edged her hands towards the clump. It squawked and fluttered away.

It was a young galah.

"Must have fallen out of a nest in that tree." Andy glanced up the cracked, grey trunk to the hollow branches at the top. Inside would be just the place for a galah's nest. "Is it hurt?"

"I don't think so," said Kate. "It's just too young to fly."

"It's scared. Look at its heart beating against its chest."

"It'll die if we leave it here."

"Probably die anyway. Wild animals always die in captivity."

"They do not!"

"Mostly. Remember that swan with a broken wing that we kept in the old chook shed? It died. And Peter Rabbit...and that magpie the cat caught, and Squeak, and..."

"We have to give it a chance!" Kate's chin lifted and her mouth set in a straight line. "I'm taking it home."

Andy grinned at her. "I knew you would."

The galah screeched and tried to bite Kate's fingers. She tucked it inside her jacket and pulled the zipper up.

"Quick, Andy. Give us a leg-up."

She held Silver's reins with one hand and pressed the other against her chest to keep the little bird still. Andy helped her scramble into the saddle, and she set off across the paddocks.

Silver clopped home past the cow shed and the machinery sheds and the chooks, scratching and clucking in their run. She pricked up her ears and whickered to Dad's big bay horse, waiting at the gate.

Kate peeped inside her jacket. In the warmth and darkness the baby galah was quiet.

"It's all right, little one," she whispered. "I'll look after you. We'll be friends. You can be my pet for the Pet Show!"

4

Normie

"THERE'S a cage in the old stable," said Andy. The stable, too old and tumbledown now for horses, was filled with treasure from years gone by. Kerosene lamps, rusted rabbit traps, horse harness, horseshoes, an old buggy, a tin trunk full of faded photographs...and a large, old-fashioned parrot cage. It was dark inside the stable and it smelt of dust and old leather.

Andy rummaged through the treasure. "Here it is!"

At that moment Normie Bright walked past the stable. Normie was Dad's right-hand man on the farm and he had been there ever since Kate and Andy could remember. He stopped and scratched his thatch of white hair.

"Need a hand, young feller?" Normie helped Andy haul the cage out into the sunlight.

"There y'are, young feller-me-lad. Good-oh, eh?

Got something to put in it, have you?'' He pulled his hooked beak of a nose, then reached into his pocket for two extra-strong peppermints. "See how tough y'are." He gave them each a peppermint, winked a beady eye, and went on his way.

"Thanks, Normie!" Kate and Andy sucked on the burning hot peppermints until tears came to their eyes.

The cage was covered with cobwebs and sparrow droppings. "Looks a bit dirty," said Andy, "but it's nice and big. Let's take it up to the front lawn and clean it out."

When the cage was ready Kate lifted the galah from inside her jacket. It blinked in the sunlight. She eased it inside, through a small doorway.

The bird's claws scratched against the metal floor. Terrified, it flapped and squawked and battered against its strange, hard prison. Downy pink and grey feathers floated into the air.

"Stop it! Stop it!" cried Kate, her hands over her mouth.

"He'll settle down soon," said Andy.

"He'll hurt himself!"

"He'll get used to it."

"He won't!"

Kate dived her hand through the doorway, grabbed the panic-stricken bird, and glared defiantly at Andy. "He can't live in a cage!"

"All right! Stop shouting. And don't *cry*, Kate!"

She looked down at the bundle she clutched and sniffed back her tears. They had made tracks down her cheeks, powdered with dust from the stable. She

wiped her nose on her shoulder and whispered, "He just wants a nice soft nest in a hollow tree."

"How can we make a nest like that? Gee, you're dumb sometimes." Andy hooked his thumbs into his jeans and kicked his riding boot. "I know! Get a towel from the linen cupboard. Better be an old one!" He was already running towards the garage.

When Kate returned, Andy had found a deep cardboard box. He tucked the towel into the bottom and sat back on his heels, satisifed.

"There. It's dark inside, like a hollow tree, and it'll be soft and warm."

Kate lowered the galah into its new nest and watched anxiously. It squatted on the towel. Its eyelids slid up over its eyes and it did not move.

"I hope he's not sick," she said. "Why is he so quiet?"

"He's tired," said Andy. "I bet you would be too. Let's carry his box to the front verandah so he can have a sleep."

The verandah was long and wide. It was enclosed with gauze wire to keep out flies and mosquitoes as well as the summer sun. Wisteria and yellow roses climbed up its wooden posts and along the corrugated iron roof of the old house. A cane sofa and two cane chairs with yellow cushions sat on the verandah.

"There you are!" Mum poked her head through the doorway. "Where have you been? I've been looking for you."

"Come and see what I found!"

"Ka-tie? What is it this time?" Mum stopped to pick up a skipping rope which lay like a snake across her path. "How many times have I told you not to leave your skipping rope lying around? There's a proper place for. . ."

"Yes, I know, but come and look!" Kate grabbed Mum's hand and dragged her towards the box.

"What a scrawny little bundle!" said Mum, peering at the galah. "Is it hurt?"

"Looks like a young one to me," said a slow, deep voice behind them.

"Dad!"

Kate wrapped her arms around her father's middle and looked up at his lined, sun-browned face. "Isn't he beautiful? We found him in Dead Tree paddock. He'd fallen out of his nest."

Dad patted her smooth brown head and smiled. "What are you going to call him?"

Kate looked at the galah and her frown changed to a wide grin. "Guess!"

Everyone leant over the box. A pink face with shiny round eyes, a hooked nose and a thatch of white hair stared back at them.

They all said it at once.

"NORMIE!"

"He looks just like Normie Bright and he's going to be my pet for the Pet Show," said Kate.

"Katie, you know how often your pets die." Mum ran her fingers through her hair and sighed. "If he does survive he can't stay on my front verandah for ever."

"Why not?" demanded Kate.

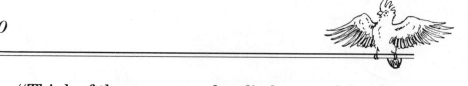

"Think of the mess once he climbs out of that box. All over my yellow cushions! I've told you often enough, Katie. . ."

"There's a proper place for everthing."

"That's right. He can live in a cage."

"No!"

"Be sensible, Katie. It would be dangerous as well as untidy to leave him out here. You know how the cat loves to get in. If anyone left the door open, just once, she'd be in as quick as lightning. And that would be the end of Normie."

Kate thought how often she had seen Tiger, their cat, pouncing on sparrows and pigeons. Tiger was well fed, never hungry, but nothing would ever stop her hunting. Often she left the feathers of her victims on the door mat.

Kate looked at the baby galah and shivered.

5

"He can't do anything..."

A FLOCK of galahs flew over the house, making their soft whistle-and-flute music in the morning light. Kate stretched like a cat in her bed, dreaming of Normie.

Normie! Suddenly she was wide awake.

She pattered along the hall in her bare feet. The house creaked. In the sitting room, chintz-covered chairs sat like statues around an empty fireplace. She hurried past and through double glass doors to the front verandah.

The cardboard box sat at the far end of the verandah, where the eastern sun already lapped across the wooden boards.

Please be alive! she wished. Her heart beat fast, as she tiptoed to the box and peered in.

There he was, huddled in a corner. His white-topped head rested on his breast and he was quite still.

"Normie?"

Kate's fingers trembled as she reached down to touch him. He was warm! He opened a sleepy eye and shuffled on his towel nest.

"Hullo, Normie."

Kate's voice shook with relief. She eased both hands around the bird's folded wings and lifted him out of the box. This time he did not try to bite. He bent his head and nibbled her fingers. She could feel his bobbly tongue.

"Ooh, that tickles!" she laughed.

She sat on the floor and made a circle with her legs. She put Normie inside the circle and slowly, watching, let go his wings.

He plumped out his feathers, settled them again, then hopped onto Kate's bare leg and shuffled sideways onto her knee.

"Ow! Your claws are sharp!"

Kate did not dare move her leg.

"Are you hungry?"

She slid her hand into the box, grabbed some sunflower seeds, and held them out to him on the palm of her hand.

He turned his head to one side and considered them for a moment. Then he dipped into the seeds and tried to crack one with his hooked beak, like a grown-up galah.

"He won't be eating that stuff for a while," came a voice from outside.

Normie Bright set a bucket of milk, still frothy from the cow, on the step. He peered through the gauze wire, his head on one side, like the bird.

"Porridge is what he needs — warm and mushy,

with honey in it. You'll have to squeeze it down his throat, like his mother would."

"How?" asked Kate.

Normie ruffled his hair and chuckled. "Ya dad's horse-drenching syringe. Just the thing."

He bent to pick up the bucket, then looked up. "And gum leaves."

"What?" Kate frowned.

"Gum leaves. Not to eat, ya duffer! He's not a bloomin' koala. Galahs line their nests with gum leaves. It'll make him feel more at home. See ya, little Kate." Normie trudged away to the kitchen door with the milk.

Kate stroked the bird's head with her finger. "We'll be friends, Normie. I'll teach you to talk and sit on my shoulder and ride on the handlebars of my bike. You'll be the best pet at the Pet Show. Wait till I tell the kids at school tomorrow!"

* * *

The next morning Kate bounced out of bed.

"What are you so cheerful about?" said Andy. "It's Monday."

"Have to feed Normie before school." She hop-step-and-jumped her way to the kitchen to make the baby galah's morning porridge.

Three quarters of an hour later Mum called, "Hurry up, Kate! You'll be late for school."

"Coming!" She tucked the galah into his nest and tickled the back of his head.

"Katie! How many times do I have to tell you?"

"Coming, Mum."

Kate pulled on her red-checked dress and brushed her hair into pigtails and gulped down a bowlful of cornflakes. The kitchen door banged behind her.

"Wait for me, Andy!"

She stopped to glance at her tadpoles in their milk-bucket aquarium, noted that all but three had grown legs, then hopped onto her bike and pedalled down the drive to catch the school bus at the front gate of the farm.

This morning the cows, fat as sea lions and shiny black, grazed near the road.

"Hullo cows!" Kate called.

They lifted their heads to her, then dropped them back into the silvery grass and swished their tails against the flies.

"Look out, Andy!"

A magpie dropped like a dart from the overhanging branch of a gum tree. Andy ducked and yelled. Centimetres from his head, the angry bird pulled out of the dive and whirred back up to its nest. It glowered down its beak at the intruders.

"What are you laughing at?" Andy wanted to know.

"Nearly got you!"

Kate felt like laughing. Everything seemed funny and shiny and happy this morning. Even school would be fun.

*　　*　　*

Everyone sat cross-legged on the green carpet. At last Mr Lodge looked up from marking the register and asked, "Who has some news this morning?"

Kate's hand shot up.

"Yes, Kate?"

She stood up, twisting her pigtail.

"On Saturday my brother and I found a baby galah. It had fallen out of its nest. I took it home and we made a nest in a cardboard box and now it's my pet. Any questions or comments?"

"What's its name?" asked Lucy.

"Normie."

"Can he talk yet?" asked Sharon.

"Not yet."

"Does he sit on your shoulder?" asked Matthew.

"Not yet."

"My budgie turns somersaults on his swing," said Harry, who was in Infants. "Can your galah do that?"

"No."

"What *can* he do?" said Cynthia.

"He can't do *anything*," Michelle said. "What a boring pet!"

Kate sat down. News time droned on, but she did not listen. Boring pet! We'll show them. Normie will be the best pet in the Pet Show. He'll sit on my shoulder and fly loop-the-loops and . . . She stopped picking her fingernail and smiled to herself. Maybe I can teach him that song that Dad sings. "K-K-K-Katie, K-K-K-Katie, You're the only g-g-g-girl that . . ."

"Kate!"

She jumped, and stared at her teacher like a frightened owl.

"Dreaming again, are we?"

Lucy caught her eye and winked. Kate returned a flicker of a smile and decided she would let Normie sit on Lucy's shoulder too.

6

Escape from a Tiger

"KATIE? Where are you going?" Mum looked up from shelling peas at the kitchen table. "To play with Normie."

"What about unpacking your school case?"

"Later."

"What about your homework? How many times have I. . .?"

"Later, Mum."

"I could do with a hand in the sheep yards," said Dad, draining his mug of tea.

"Da-ad. Not today."

"It's not fair!" Andy followed his sister into the kitchen and slammed the door behind him. "I've fed the chooks every day since you got that galah. That's *two weeks*. It's *your* turn, Kate."

"Please, Andy! Just till after the Pet Show. I'll do *all* your jobs for a month after that. I have so much to teach Normie, and there's only a week to go."

Kate sidled out the door and disappeared to the verandah.

*   *   *

Normie had grown. He was plumper and his tail feathers were longer. His crest looked whiter and his chest pinker as his grey baby feathers fell out. He had stopped crying for Kate to squeeze porridge from Dad's horse-drenching syringe down his throat. Now he cracked birdseed with his strong, hooked beak and nibbled titbits that Kate scrounged for him. He loved Anzac biscuits best of all.

Sometimes wild galahs chased each other in a joyful race over the house, screeching and swerving. Then Normie flapped to the edge of the verandah and called to them, but they did not hear.

This afternoon Kate found him perched on his cardboard box, busily combing his feathers with his beak.

"Hullo, Normie," she said, reaching for a broom propped against the wall.

"*'Ullo Normie,*" he replied. He turned his head to one side and watched her with an eye as round and polished as a dewdrop.

"*Wheeoowhee!*"

Dad's whistling the dogs, Kate said to herself as she swept up birdseed. He must be going to the sheep yards. She felt mean for not helping him. Outside, Sparkie, Dad's black and tan kelpie, pricked her ears and hopped on her hind legs and looked for her master. But he was nowhere to be seen.

"*Wheeoowhee!*"

Sparkie barked and whined. She scratched against the gauze wire of the verandah and peered in with her head on one side.

"Dad's not in here, Sparkie." Kate leant on the broom and looked around, puzzled. Then her mouth fell open and she stared in disbelief.

"Normie? Is it *you?*"

"*Wheeoowhee!*" came Normie's cheeky reply.

"You clever boy! You tricked us! We thought it was Dad!"

Kate laughed and clapped her hands. She reached out and Normie climbed onto her finger. He shuffled sideways up her arm and perched on her shoulder.

"I love you, Normie. Don't let anything happen to you, ever."

Kate rubbed her cheek against his face. He nibbled

her ear and worked at undoing the red ribbon which tied her pigtail.

"Off you go, you pest. I have to finish cleaning up, or Mum will say you have to go in a cage."

She swept the floor and wiped bird droppings from the cane furniture. (The yellow cushions had been stacked away in the spare room.)

Normie waddled away, his toenails click-clicking on the wooden boards. He eyed the verandah door and, having nothing better to do, tore at its white-painted frame with his beak. The door had jammed slightly open — just enough for an inquisitive galah to poke his head through and squeeze quietly outside.

In the wisteria, among the heavy bunches of purple blossom, Tiger the cat slunk along a branch, hunting sparrows. She looked down at the young galah nibbling onion weed in the lawn. Her tail twitched. Her eyes gleamed yellow.

"Aach! Aach! Aach!"

Kate swung around to see Tiger's back arched over something flapping on the lawn. Then she saw the open door and her insides seemed to somersault.

"Normie!"

She dropped the broom, dashed outside, and threw herself onto the flurry of fur and feathers.

"Tiger, let go!"

She wrenched open the cat's jaws and the galah dropped to the ground.

"Go away! I hate you!"

Kate, who loved animals, kicked at the cat in fury. Tiger galloped away with her tail in a spiky curve. Normie lay still on the grass.

"No!" Kate whispered. "Oh, *no!*"

She gathered the bedraggled body into her hands, rocked it against her chest, and sobbed.

"What happened?" Andy ran from the house.

"Tiger got Normie."

"Is he all right?"

Kate sniffed and looked down at a dried clot of blood on Normie's white crest. Two tail-feathers were missing. His eyes were closed. But his little heart pattered in her hands.

"He's still alive!"

She stroked his feathers with her finger. Suddenly he opened his eyes, looked about, and started to nibble her hands. She laughed, though the tears still ran down her cheeks.

"Phew," sighed Andy. "That was a close shave. Hope he doesn't die of shock. Jason Thomas said a cat frightened his budgie to death, while it was still in its cage."

Normie proved he was tougher than any caged budgie. He fluffed out his feathers, preened what was left of his tail, and ate a piece of Anzac biscuit from Kate's pocket. Apart from the wound on his head, which Kate bathed with disinfectant, he soon looked his own chirpy self again.

That night Kate smiled in her sleep. She dreamt that Normie was sitting in the old dead tree where he was born, telling all the other galahs how he escaped from a tiger.

7

"Clip his wings . . ."

"**L**UCY, guess what!" Kate ran up the path from the school gate. "We've taught Normie to fly!" "You should have seen him!" said Andy. "Just like Kate learning to ride a bike. He didn't know how to stop, so he flew straight into a tree!" Andy flapped his arms and flew a wobbly path into a pepper tree. Lucy laughed.

"He crash-landed on Andy's hat," said Kate. "Pow! He was flapping and clawing, trying to keep his balance, and Andy was squawking like a hundred galahs. Then he sat up and preened his feathers, as if he'd been flying for years!"

"You're *stupid!*"

Kate jumped and looked over her shoulder. Michelle lumbered towards her, zinging a yo-yo up and down. Kate forgot to shut her mouth.

"Whatcha think he'll do now? He'll fly away, of

course, and that's the last you'll see of him. *Flycatcher.*"

"No he won't! He's my friend."

"He's my frie-nd," Michelle mimicked in a teasing, sing-song voice. "Course he will. He'll go with the wild galahs. You should clip his wings. That's what my dad says. Clip their wings and they can never fly."

She spun her yo-yo over the back of her hand, then flicked it at Kate.

"Who wants to hear about a boring galah, anyway? We've got much better pets for the Pet Show."

She walked away arm in arm with Cynthia and Sharon.

In school, Kate kept thinking of what Michelle had said. Would Normie fly away? Other pets did not run away from their owners.

She could not concentrate on her work. Mr Lodge got cross and told her to stop daydreaming.

* * *

It was mail day. Dad sat at the kitchen table with a pot of tea and a pile of newspapers and letters scattered around him. Normie Bright leant his elbows on the table and held a steaming mug between his brown, veiny hands. Kate and Andy clattered into the kitchen and took an apple each from the fruit bowl.

"Dad," mumbled Kate, wiping apple juice from her chin, "what does it mean to 'clip a bird's wings'?"

"You cut one wing short so the bird can't fly," Dad answered. "Some people do it to their pets."

"That's cruel!"

"It is," agreed Dad from behind his newspaper. "They only cut the feathers, though. It doesn't hurt."

"You'd never do that to Normie, would you?" Normie Bright glanced at Kate, and his hooked nose looked as fierce as a hawk's.

"Never!"

"Free as the air, that's what birds are made to be." Normie slurped his tea.

Kate munched her apple. "Michelle says Normie will fly away."

Normie Bright reached for his hat and stood up. "People like Michelle aren't worth botherin' about, little Kate. Thanks for the tea, Mrs Harman."

Mum stood at the sink, washing silver beet from the garden. She turned to Kate. "I'm sure he won't fly away. Like Normie says, don't listen to Michelle. But you could put him in a cage, to be safe."

"But Mum, he hates cages!"

"We could fix him up a nice big one in the garden. . .for his own good, Katie. I've told you often enough, it's dangerous outside. He could be hit by a car. Or attacked by a hawk. You know how Tiger nearly got him. She'll try again if she gets the chance."

Kate thought of Normie snuggling into her shoulder and nibbling her hair. Normie perched on the handlebars of her bike, with his feathers ruffling in the wind. Normie on her head, shrieking "*'Owzat!*" when she and Andy and Dad played cricket together. Normie flying around the horse paddock and swooping down to her when she called. He *couldn't* live in a cage.

"But...but...I've taught him to fly!" Kate ran out of the room.

The following afternoon Kate came home from school feeling angry.

"That Michelle!" she told Normie. "Do you know what she said today?"

"*'Owzat!*" Normie squawked, and hopped up and down on her shoulder.

"No!"

Kate smiled and gave him a piece of her Anzac biscuit. Then the smile faded and her brown eyes gleamed with tears. They filled like lakes before they spilt over and splodged down her cheeks.

"She called me Teacher's Pet. Just because I got a Terrific Effort sticker for my natural science project. She kept whispering 'Tea-cher's Pe-et, Tea-cher's Pe-et' so everyone could hear except Mr Lodge. So Andy called her 'Toad Features' and then Mr Lodge heard and Andy had to stay in at lunch-time and then no-one, except Lucy, would play with me and it was awful. Why does she have to be so mean?"

Normie clucked and nibbled her ear.

"We'll show her! Let's practise your landings for the Pet Show."

Clouds had painted the sky dark silver-grey, like pewter. A hot wind blew from the north.

"There's a storm coming," said Kate.

Normie was excited. He turned and swooped like a piece of paper blowing in the wind, now pink, now grey.

"Nor-mie."

Kate called and the galah flew back to her. His claws gripped her hair and he landed neatly on her head.

"Good boy. We'd better go inside. It's going to pour."

Thunder growled.

Suddenly a screaming cloud of wild galahs swept into the pewter sky. They *whooshed* past like a brilliant, noisy kaleidoscope and lifted, shattering into a hundred pieces, to settle in the mahogany gum which soared highest of all the trees in the garden.

Normie gave one cry and sprang from Kate's head . . .

8

"I told you so . . ."

"**N**ORMIE!" screamed Kate.
He flew away from her and disappeared into the crowd of wild galahs in the tree.

Kate ran on tiptoes to the foot of the tree. She did not dare to call out in case she frightened them away. She shielded her eyes and scanned the rows of white-crested, pink-breasted, grey-backed birds. They jostled and chattered on their branches and they all looked exactly the same.

The wind whipped to the south-west and blew the first cold drops of rain. The gum tree swayed and roared high above her head. Please come back, she prayed. Don't fly away!

All at once the galahs sprang from the tree and swooped like a giant pink and grey kite before the wind. Kate heard the *whoosh* of their wings and the crescendo of their screeching. They turned their breasts in a flash of pink and headed into the blackening sky.

At the tail of the galah kite one smaller bird beat his wings into the wind.

Wait for me! he seemed to say.

"Normie! Come back!"

Kate raced across the lawn, her eyes fixed on the diminishing flock of birds. She slipped on the gravel drive and skidded onto her knees. She picked herself up and hurdled over the long grass on the other side of the drive, until she reached the white post-and-rail fence which surrounded the garden.

Kate beat her fists on the fence and shouted, "Come back!"

Rain pelted against her back and drenched her cotton dress. The birds dissolved into the murky sky. She dropped her head onto the railing and howled.

"In the midst of the storm and the hurricane, what are you doing, little Kate?" Normie Bright shook her by the shoulders. Rain dripped from his sou'wester hat onto his nose, and his oilskin coat flapped around his ankles.

"Normie's gone," she sobbed.

"It won't help to drown yourself, Kate. Come in out of the wet." Normie grabbed her hand and they hurried through the stinging rain to the house. He opened the back door and pushed her inside. "Don't worry, little Kate. He'll be all right."

"What's the matter?" said Andy in the warm kitchen.

"You'd better get out of those wet things," said Dad, handing her his jumper.

"Let me rub your hair dry," said Mum, a towel slung between her hands.

"What's the matter?" Andy asked again.

"Normie's gone."

Kate shivered. She peeled off her dripping clothes and pulled on Dad's thick navy-blue jumper. She backed against the stove and pressed her hands against its warm door. She took a shuddering breath and sighed.

"We were practising and the storm came and some wild galahs flew over, making such a din, and Normie. . .Normie flew away." Her voice wavered. "I called and called but he wouldn't come back."

"Katie. . ." Mum hugged her. "I told you it was dangerous for him outside."

"He'll come back," said Dad. "He's just excited by the storm."

"But it's nearly dark!" whispered Kate. She stared out the kitchen window at the thrashing garden. "He'll be so wet and cold."

"Probably snug in a hollow tree," said Andy.

"He's only little and he's never been out before. He couldn't fly home against that wind."

As she spoke, the wind pounded the rain even harder onto the iron roof.

"You told me galahs are really strong fliers," said Andy. "Let's leave the verandah door open in case he comes home tonight."

*   *   *

Kate lay in bed and listened to the rain drumming on the roof. Usually she loved the sound, but tonight she longed to hear the peaceful dripping and gurgling that signalled the end of a storm. A flash of lightning lit the old pine tree as it tossed and bowed in the wind. What's happening to the topknot pigeons in their nest? she wondered. Where's Normie? Is he wet and shivering on a branch? Is he lying in a ditch? Is he lost? She rolled her pillow around her ears and cried.

*   *   *

When Kate opened her eyes in the morning the clouds had blown away. The sky was washed-out blue. A cold south-westerly wind blew and the verandah door banged monotonously. Then Kate remembered — they had left it open for Normie. She had a sinking feeling inside that made her think she could not eat any breakfast.

She searched the verandah and the garden. Normie was not there.

In the playground at school everyone talked about the Pet Show.

"Only two more days!" said Matthew. He grinned, and his ears stuck out.

"Mum says I can have a new mirror for my budgie's cage," Harry told Brian.

"I've brushed Pancho for half an hour every day," said Brian. "I'm going to plait his mane and tail and polish his hooves with shoe polish. You can have a ride."

Michelle flicked her yo-yo down and watched it climb back up its string. "Tess will do anything for me. She knows my whistles for 'Sit' and 'Stay' and 'Come Here'," she boasted.

"I've painted Nibs's hutch," said Lucy, hopping along the hopscotch squares. At the end she jumped, turned, and looked at Kate. "Will Normie talk for us? Will you let him sit on my shoulder?"

Kate drew a circle on the ground with her shoe. She felt everyone looking at her. Tears flooded her eyes.

"Normie's gone," she whispered.

"What?"

"Oh, no!"

"What happened?"

The children crowded around her.

"Flew away, did he? *I told ya so!*"

"Shut up, Michelle!" said Andy.

"He's probably been hit by a car," Michelle continued. "Y'see dead galahs by the road all the time. He couldn't live in the wild, anyway."

"Why not?" Kate shouted. "Of course he could!"

"Pet budgies can't. They can't find food, and the wild budgerigars kill them."

"How do you know? You're just making it up. It's not true! Anyway, Normie's not a budgie — he's a galah."

The bell rang.

Don't let him be dead, Kate prayed as she followed the others to line up. Please keep him safe. I don't care about the Pet Show. I don't care about Michelle. She can call me what she likes. Just let Normie be all right!

9

Kate's Dream

"HAS HE come back?"

Mum shook her head. "Sorry, Darling."

Kate dropped her school case on the kitchen floor and turned away.

"Help me get Baa ready for the Pet Show," said Andy. "I have to pull some grass seeds out of her wool."

"I think I'll go for a ride on my bike."

Kate rode along the drive in the direction Normie and the galahs had flown. She did not expect to find him, but she felt better to be doing something. The bike plunged through the puddles in the road, splashing mud onto her legs. The magpie in its gum tree dive-bombed her, but she shouted so angrily that it flew away in surprise.

At the front gate she turned and pedalled along the main road.

Suddenly her stomach lurched. A dead galah lay

in the gravel, flung aside by a rushing car. Kate leapt off her bike and let it crash to the ground.

Could it be Normie?

Gently, she gathered the bird into her hands. Its head flopped over her fingers and its soft pink feathers stirred in the breeze. It wasn't Normie. There were no grey baby feathers. It had the clear colours of a full-grown galah. But she remembered what Michelle had said. Would Normie be hit by a car too? Could he find enough to eat? Would the other galahs attack him?

She pushed home into a cold headwind.

* * *

That night Kate dreamt of gigantic galahs flapping in her face, screaming at her, scratching her. She dreamt she was in a car. It hurtled through a flock of galahs on the road. The birds sprang up in alarm. *Thunk! Thunk!* They hit the bonnet, the wheels, the windscreen. Their bodies spun away in flurries of feathers. Kate moaned and tossed in her sleep.

Just before dawn she had a different dream. It was quiet and clear and so real that when she woke up she was confused to find herself in bed.

There was a pine forest. There was a fence and a gate and, in between, a huge old red-gum strainer post. The fence wires had been strained so tightly around the post they cut into the wood. Its centre had begun to rot, leaving a hollow in the top.

A galah sat in the hollow. It tried to fly but it could not. It kept beating its wings and lifting off the post, then falling back again.

Kate's eyes opened wide in the dark. She saw the morning star and watched the sky beginning to pale. I know that pine forest, she thought. I've seen that gate and that strainer post. Is that where Normie is? Why can't he fly home?

Don't be silly, Kate. It's only a dream. The voices of Mum and Dad and Andy and Mr Lodge echoed in her mind.

It wouldn't hurt to look, little Kate, said another familiar voice.

I can ride Silver to that spot, she said to herself. I know where it is. I'll wake Andy.

No. It's just a dream, he'd say. You're such a dreamer, Kate.

She sighed. Dreams weren't real. She turned on her side and squeezed her eyes shut. It all came back. The forest, the fence, the gate, the strainer post, the galah struggling.

Why couldn't he fly?

Go, little Kate, whispered Normie Bright.

She sat up. I *will* go, she decided. By myself.

Kate slid out of bed, glancing at Andy's sleeping shadow. She dressed and tiptoed in the semi-darkness to the kitchen, carrying her squeaky riding boots.

She packed an emergency kit — a plastic drink container filled with water, one of Dad's handkerchiefs from the laundry basket, to tie up a broken wing or a cut leg, and two Anzac biscuits.

Mum's shopping pad and pen hung on the wall beside the fridge. Kate tore off a page and wrote, "Gone to look for Normie. Back soon." She left it on the kitchen table under the sugar bowl.

* * *

Silver pranced and tossed her head and snorted in the tingling air. The earth smelt damp and clean after the rain. The fiery face of the sun rose in the east and for a moment Kate forgot her worries. It was a fresh, new morning — and she had it all to herself. She breathed deeply and leant forward to pat Silver's neck.

They trotted across the dry creek bed and around the wheat crop in the next paddock. Two quail whirred from the stalks and made Silver jump. They clopped across the main road and continued north through Dead Tree paddock, where Kate had found Normie. They passed a windmill, with its giant vanes creaking in the morning breeze. They rode over the bank of a dam, where teal ducks swam on the ruffled water.

The pine forest loomed, dark and quiet. A fence disappeared into the trees.

Silver walked along a sandy sheep track beside the fence. Kate ducked beneath the low branches of the pine trees. Twigs scratched her face; barbed wire in the fence clawed at her jeans.

The trees thinned and she could see a strainer post in the corner of the paddock. Her heart beat faster.

Was that the spot?

No. There was no gate.

She tried to remember. If she turned right along the new fence she would come to a gate at the next corner. Clear of the trees now, she cantered to the gate.

It was exactly like the dream. The fence, the gate, the strainer post — and something which made Kate's heart hammer. There, fluttering frantically, was the galah.

Overhead, a wedge-tailed eagle circled in search of prey.

Kate hardly dared to breathe. She kicked Silver, and the pony flattened her ears and spurted forward.

"Normie! It *is* you!"

She threw herself from Silver's back and hugged the galah between her hands.

He whistled softly and nibbled her hair.

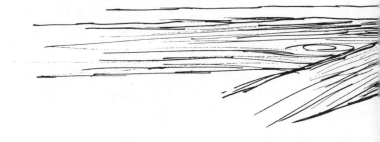

"Oh Normie, what's happened to you?"

The galah's leg was tangled in a coil of fencing wire, left in the top of the post where he had landed to rest. Every time he tried to fly the wire pulled tighter. He was caught.

The wire snapped and jabbed at Kate's fingers and sprang back on Normie's leg like a trap. She gritted her teeth. If only I'd brought Dad's wire-cutters, she thought. But I can't go back for them. That wedge-tail would get Normie.

At last she managed to free him. She sucked a torn finger. Normie's leg hung bruised and bleeding. He had worn a patch of feathers off his breast.

"Poor Normie." Kate poured water into the cap of the drink container and the galah drank. She dipped Dad's handkerchief into the water and gently bathed his leg. Then she tied the handkerchief around it like a bandage.

"I brought some Anzac biscuits."

She broke off a piece and he nibbled hungrily while she crunched her share.

Kate could hardly believe it. The dream was true! She hugged the galah again and said, "Let's go home."

For the second time in his life, Normie rode home on Silver's back, nestled safely inside Kate's jacket.

* * *

Mum hurried towards Kate and Silver. "Where have been been? It's so late! Andy's gone to school already. I was so. . .*Katie!*"

A pink face with white hair and dewdrop eyes popped out of Kate's jacket.

"*'Ullo, Normie,*" it croaked.

Mum held both hands to her head. "Where did you find him? Is he all right? Come and have breakfast, both of you."

"Do I have to go to school today, Mum?" said Kate, as they walked to the house.

Mum put her arm around Kate's shoulder and hugged her. "No. You both deserve a day at home. We'll clean up that leg and bandage it and give you

both a big breakfast. Then you and Normie can have a
good rest. What a surprise you'll give everyone at the
Pet Show tomorrow!''

10

The Pet with the Happiest Owner

WHAT A procession greeted Mr Lodge and Mrs Reed, the School Inspector, on that Friday morning!

The children had assembled with their pets on the cricket field behind the school. Matthew's carpet snake, Cyril, coiled around the boy's shoulders, flicking his tongue and darting his head in the spring sunshine.

"Eek!" shrieked Lucy. "Go away! You'll scare Nibs." The grey and white rabbit twitched her nose and flicked her velvety ears in her newly-painted hutch.

Old Tess, Michelle's border collie dog, flopped in the shade of a pepper tree, panting. She had been washed and brushed until her black and white coat gleamed. She wore a new leather collar with silver studs.

Normie perched on Kate's shoulder, like a wounded soldier in pink and grey uniform. His leg was neatly bandaged with white tape. When he and Kate had arrived at school everyone had rushed up to them.

"Normie's here!"

"You found him!"

"What happened to him?"

"Look at his leg!"

Michelle said, "Imagine bringing a maimed animal to a Pet Show." But no-one took any notice of her.

"Right!" bellowed Mr Lodge.

All eyes turned to the teacher.

"Right. First I'd like to welcome Mrs Reed, our School Inspector, who has come to see our Pet Show and help me judge the prizes."

"Hooray!" The children clapped. Mrs Reed bowed her head and clasped her hands beneath her large, floral bosom.

"Right. Each of you will come forward with your pet to Mrs Reed and me and tell us all about it." Mr Lodge touched his moustache. "Let's start with . . . Anna."

Proudly — solemnly — impatiently — shyly — the children came forward to show their pets.

Baa sheep trit-trotted on polished hooves. Her black face had been washed to the tips of her black ears and her wool had been clipped and shampooed. Over her shoulders she wore a blue ribbon.

"Baa's mother died when she was a baby," said Andy. "We fed her with a bottle. She had a lamb of her own last year. She won this ribbon at the Jalandra Show."

Everyone clapped. Baa went back to grazing the cricket field.

Brian cantered Pancho around in a circle, then dismounted and walked between the pony's legs to show how quiet he was.

Sharon brought a squirmy black puppy called Buster. She held him up for the judges to see. He licked Mrs Reed's face. When she put him on the ground he chewed Mr Lodge's shoelaces.

Michelle strode forward with Tess at her heels. "Tess is a sheep dog," she said. "She knows what to do when I whistle. She only listens to me."

Michelle whistled a short, sharp note. Tess sat down. Michelle walked away, then whistled a long,

rising note. Tess trotted to her mistress, with her ears flat and her mouth smiling. Michelle whistled a note that went up in the middle and down again. Tess looked around, ears pricked. She saw Baa grazing and padded around the sheep to bring her back.

"That's called a cast," explained Michelle. The spectators watched closely. She swelled with pride.

Normie watched too, his head on one side.

In the middle of the cast, Tess heard the whistle to sit. She dropped to the ground.

"Who did that?" Michelle spun around and glared. Everyone looked at each other in surprise. Kate pressed her lips together and stared at her shoes. Normie preened.

Michelle whistled again and Tess continued the cast. Suddenly a "Come Here" whistle sounded. Tess stopped and trotted obediently back to the spectators.

"Who did that?" shouted Michelle.

Kate snorted and spluttered with laughter. Puzzled eyes turned to her and Normie.

"Sit!" whistled Normie, and Tess sat.

"Did you see that?"

"It's Normie!"

"Yeah, Normie!"

They all burst out laughing and cheering.

Michelle flushed crimson. "Get up!" she yelled.

But Normie imitated the casting whistle, so Tess took off instead.

"Stop!" Michelle's toad face was now beetroot-coloured.

The children cackled with laughter. Mr Lodge's moustache quivered and his eyes twinkled. Mrs Reed's bosom wobbled like a flummery.

"Come here!" whistled Normie. Tess ran to him. She jumped up and down in front of Kate and the galah, whining and wagging her tail.

Everyone but Michelle clapped and cheered. Michelle grabbed Tess by her collar, clipped on a lead, and tied the dog up under a pepper tree.

"After that performance, you'd better show us what else Normie can do," laughed Mr Lodge.

"Right!" said Normie, and was greeted with a fresh burst of laughter. Even Michelle had to smile.

The galah flew around the cricket field. He managed to land on Kate's head, though it was difficult with his bandaged leg. He perched on Mr Lodge's shoulder and pulled his moustache. He nibbled a biscuit from Mrs Reed's hand.

After all the pets had been shown, Mrs Reed gave out the prize ribbons.

"The prize for the smallest pet," she announced. "Anna's mouse, Pinkie."

Anna wiped her hand on her dress and took the ribbon.

"The naughtiest pet. Buster!"

Sharon walked forward, with Buster wriggling under her arm.

"The scariest pet. Matthew's snake, Cyril. Don't bring him near me!

"The most obedient pet. Michelle's Tess. Even though she didn't know *who* to obey!"

The children laughed again. Michelle scowled.

Mrs Reed continued through the list of prizes. Brian and Andy shared the prize for the best presented pet. Lucy won the prize for the best house for a pet.

Then Mrs Reed announced, "The funniest pet. Normie!"

"May I add," called Mrs Reed over the cheering and applause, "that after his narrow escapes, and the fact that he nearly wasn't here today, I would like to make a special award." Mrs Reed paused. "I judge Normie to be. . ." She paused again. "The pet with the happiest owner!"

"Hooray!" shouted the children of Doongara Primary School.

Kate smiled so much her cheeks ached. She was glad Normie had made everyone laugh. She was glad he had played such a good trick on Michelle.

But Normie Bright was right. People like Michelle weren't worth bothering about. She had Normie.

The pet with the happiest owner. Kate smiled. . .and silently agreed.

The End